Alex DèLarge

I0670162

Naughty Shorts

The Waitress

THE
WAITRESS

Written by

Alex DèLarge

Blue **B**unny **A**gency
London

Copyright

THE WAITRESS

First of adult short stories in the series Adult bedtime "Naughty Shorts" stories

www.BlueBunny.Agency

Publishers Note:
This work is fiction any association to names, places and incidents is the imagination of the Author.
Any resemblance to actual people, living or dead is completely coincidental.

ISBN: 978-0-9934180-1-3

This edition published in November 2015

by The Blue Bunny Agency

www.BlueBunny.Agency

Illustrations by Dreamstime.com

Chapters

Dedication

To Marion...

...for always believing in me.

Preface

"The Waitress" is a humorous adult bed-

time story!

This is the first book in the

series..."Naughty Shorts".

Are you sitting comfortably?

Are you dressed appropriately...?!

...then let's begin!

Chapter One – Alex

Pay-day wasn't something Alex looked forward to, as he largely ignored his financial situation.

As long as is debit card worked, his paycheck arrived as scheduled and he paid his credit card on time, life was good.

Good, but boring...IT work means long, unfulfilling hours of abject boredom, sharing each day with tedious co-workers.

Okay, so what...we are doing something about that tonight...being Friday, Alex thought.

Alex lives alone (figures, right?) in a crumbling old house close to the local University campus.

Bequeathed to him that year, by an eccentric Uncle, it still had his nick-knacks around the place. Although Alex had a clear out of stuff from the closets, attic and basement, Alex decided not to ditch everything, as it would leave the house bare and spooky...

after all, his Uncle left some comfortable furniture.

Keys in hand, Alex opened the front door and looked back...not so welcoming, so he put on the porch and hallway lights.

His Aston Martin (another neglected inheritance, from Uncle) barked into life. Maybe a nice Italian supper – on my own - but maybe it will be lively with families catching-up, he thought.

Chapter Two – My Name is Daisy

Although still busy, the restaurant was starting to thin-out, as families with younger children started to make moves to return home.

Great, a corner booth, he thought, as he was shown to his table. I'll be able to see what's going on.

"My name is Daisy and I'll be your server tonight"…a young, tired looking woman stood poised with pen and note pad, ready to take

Alex's order. Her uniform name-badge confirmed her introduction "My name is DAISY".

"Groovy", Alex blurted out. Note to self, he thought, stop saying "groovy".

Surprisingly, Daisy responded with an amused smile.

"I can see you need a few minutes to get acquainted with the menu...I'll be back with some water..."

As smooth as silk, she headed to the kitchen.

An interesting start, thought Alex...

Now glad he put the effort to select his favorite shirt, clean Jeans and Bruno Magli shoes...the only designer-name in his wardrobe.

While browsing the menu, Alex saw Daisy flit from table to table…clearing tables here and settling up cheques there.

There is a girl who focuses on her tips, he concluded.

"Okay hun', how are we going with the menu?"

Alex surprised himself by demanding…

"A glass of Red and today's special, please…no starter".

"Very decisive", slurred Daisy in a seductive tone.

"Your wish is my command", she added, as she scribbled furiously.

This is turning out to be a military operation, Alex thought…time to slow things down…

"…unless you recommend an alternative…?"

"The meatballs are my favorite…spicy and home-made…the special is nearly gone, as it was a family favorite, tonight", she added.

"Meatballs it is – the spicier the better!", said Alex.

"Well, okay then.." responded Daisy, with her winning smile and sexy tone.

Now full of Meatballs, followed by Alex's favorite - cheese and crackers - Alex's attention returned to Daisy's unbridled energy.

Chapter Three – Bad Dog

Just then, Alex noted a commotion at the restaurant entrance.

Taking advantage of customers leaving, a boisterous Staffordshire terrier burst in, darting underneath tables, causing Daisy to drop a large tray of dirty dishes.

"Butch", she shouted, how did you get free?"

"You own this animal?", barked the restaurant owner, at Daisy.

"Kinda, I'm looking after him for a friend", said Daisy, by then seemingly torn between clearing the mess and capturing the dog.

Alex found himself shouting "I'll get him, I have a collar and lead in my car."

Wow, where did that one come from, Alex thought, as he rushed out to the Aston.

Uncle had a - long since passed - dog...for some reason the collar and leash was still in the glove box.

Chasing down the excited animal wasn't easy, but Alex managed to slip on the collar and calm him down at his table, while order returned to the restaurant.

Fortunately, for Daisy, the whole event was seen as amusing interlude, by the remaining customers.

Mess and mayhem, now clear, Daisy returned to thank Alex.

"You saved the day", said Daisy, grinning with relief.

The meatballs must have unleashed your super-strength... Butch is a real handful..." she added.

"...If you don't mind hanging out for 30-minutes, until my shift ends, then I can sort Butch out...I'll bring you another drink, to say thank you".

"Sure" Alex replied, before thinking...

Chapter Four – Nice car

"Nice car", said Daisy, as Alex settled Butch behind the front seat.

"If you saw the maintenance bill, you would choose a Toyota", Alex quipped.

"What's the story with Butch?" Alex asked, as he pulled away from the Restaurant.

"Oh, just looking after him, while the owners take a weekend away…he must have got loose".

"Well, I have a kennel at the back of my Garage, which is secure and warm, how about we set Butch up there, then you have no more worries he will escape?

I have no food, but I'm sure we can sort that out"

"That's great – thank you!"…Looks like the meatballs have unlocked a sharp brain!"

"If we can call by the owner's place, I can grab a couple of cans of dog food, then we could swing by my apartment, where I can de-waitress myself"!...Daisy added.

Dog food in the boot, Daisy climbs back in the car – now changed into Black high heeled shoes (hmmmm…interesting), Black sweat pants and Black hoodie (Hmmmm…the Ninja student look!)

Old blankets re-purposed as Butch's new bed, they head to Alex's house, for some adult beverages.

"You make the drinks and I'll powder my nose", Daisy said

"Top of the stairs, first left" Alex replied.

Deciding to go sober, with the drinks – Alex prepared two Shirley Temples...

Chapter Five – I need a hand…

Now in the lounge, Alex hears Daisy shout from upstairs…

"Hey Alex, I need a hand…"

Alex panicked…had he run out of toilet paper?

"On my way", Alex called back…

Into the hallway, Alex finds himself plunged into darkness…then the lights snap-on….

Blinking, Alex looked up to see Daisy standing at the top of the stairs, legs akimbo, wearing:

- Black high heels – remembering those!

- Black stockings

- Black skimpy panties

- Black bra (with attributes which pushed the goodies in a very positive way).

"I flushed the toilet and all my clothes fell off!" stated Daisy, in a very playful voice.

Well, at least I'm off the hook with the toilet paper, thought Alex.

Alex felt he took the stairs three at a time, but his legs seem to be stuck in treacle!

Like a crazed Ninja, Daisy took Alex by the collar, shoved him through the Bedroom door (clearly she found time to do a recce of his place) and onto his bed.

Inexplicably, Alex's first thought was that he should have invested in something better than the Ikea construction project.

While he was banishing thoughts of Swedish flatpack furnishings, Daisy discarded her skimpy panties to the same place as her track pants and hoodie.

Another Ninja move put her genitals 2-inches from Alex's nose, with her hands tightly gripping his Svelvik.

Yes, Alex was still thinking Ikea.

While Alex put his mouth and tongue into appropriate action, Daisy went into a tirade of astonishing language, obviously as a result of:

- Lessons from the Italian chef or...
- A wakening of Tourette syndrome.

All this in time with gyrating her waitress-toned hips.

Unfortunately for Alex, he burst out laughing.

In his present repose, this must have flicked-on the ecstasy button, within Daisy, as she gave a final burst of Anglo/Italian and fell into a heap on the bed, shortly followed by loud snoring...sounding much like a hobo on a freight train.

Chapter Six – Alex takes stock...

Alex decided to take stock of the situation:

1. *Had a good evening in a nice restaurant – √*

2. *Played good Samaritan, rescuing a waitress from certain unemployment – √*

3. *Gave a dog a 4-star hotel – √*

4. *Played host to Gypsy Rose Lee – √*

5. *Witnessed a female sexual experience worthy of the Guinness book of world records (sex edition), for the fastest orgasm – √*

Chapter Seven - What now?

Running through his options:

1. Remove her heels, cover her up and sleep on the couch.
2. Take the dog for a walk.
3. Run screaming out of the house, never to return.
4. Call Mum for advice

Chapter Eight – Better call Mum

An open-minded woman, Alex's mum was not shy of sharing her thoughts on the matter.

"Don't be a meatball – cover the girl up, sleep on the couch and work it out in the morning".

Clearly, Alex's mum picked up on ongoing food metaphor.

Hanging up..."Typical", thought Alex, "...do the right thing..."

He dutifully removed her heels, covered her up (Daisy still snoring at the threshold of pain) and took the dog out for a walk.
At least two out of three of us ended the evening with a 'happy ending', concluded Alex.

The End

BlueBunny.Agency

By

Alex DèLarge

For the latest titles in the series of Naughty Shorts check out

www.Facebook.com/bluebunnyagency

or

www.bluebunny.agency

www.ingramcontent.com/pod-product-compliance
Lightning Source LLC
Chambersburg PA
CBHW040906120626
46551CB00006B/664